TIME OUT,
GRUMPY BUNNY!

For all the librarians who shush and share.
—J.K.F.

For Tucker.
—Love, Lucy

Text copyright © 2005 by Justine Korman Fontes
Illustrations copyright © 2005 by Lucinda McQueen

ISBN 0-439-68780-2

12 11 10 9 8 7 6 5 4 3 2   5 6 7 8 9 10/0

Printed in the U.S.A.
First printing, September 2005

TIME OUT, GRUMPY BUNNY!

by Justine Korman Fontes
Illustrated by Lucinda McQueen

SCHOLASTIC INC.

New York   Toronto   London   Auckland   Sydney
Mexico City   New Delhi   Hong Kong   Buenos Aires

Chapter 1
A Bad Morning

"Oh, worms! I'm late!"
cried Hopper O'Hare.

He ran toward school.
SMACK!
Hopper fell on his lunch!

Hopper put his mushy lunch
into his cubby.
He saw Corny, Lilac, and Marigold
put away their library books.

"Oh, more wiggly worms!" Hopper said.
"I forgot my books!"
His ears turned red.

"It's time for math,"
Mrs. Clover said.
She wrote the homework problems
on the board.

Hopper's ears turned even redder.
"I did the wrong pages!" he cried.
Mrs. Clover said, "*Shh!*"

Then she added, "Hopper, please do
the first one."
Hopper was still mad about doing
the wrong pages.
So he made a mistake.

Mrs. Clover fixed Hopper's answer.
"Oh, wiggly worms on toast!"
Hopper said. "I knew that!"

But it was too late.

Chapter 2
At the Library

Hopper looked out the window.
His ears fell.
"Mushy lunch and rain clouds,"
Hopper said. "This day is just
one long worm."

"At least it's Library Day,"
said Lilac Lapin.
Hopper smiled.
He loved Library Day.

Soon, Hopper's class lined up
in front of the library.
"Oh, crunchy carrots!" Hopper cried.
"New books!"

Mrs. Pumpkin greeted the class
at the door.
The librarian held her finger
to her lips.
She said, "*Shh!*"

Hopper found a great book.
"Hey, Corny!" he said.

Hopper forgot to whisper.

Suddenly, there was a loud *Shh!*
Mrs. Pumpkin was right behind them!

Hopper almost jumped out of his fur.

Later, Hopper and Corny waited
in line to check out books.
"Oh, worms!" Hopper said.
"This is taking too long!"
Marigold turned around.
She said, *"Shh!"*

Finally, it was Hopper's turn.
"You can't check those out yet,"
Mrs. Pumpkin said.
"You need to bring back
the old books first."

Hopper's ears turned bright red.
His face felt hot.
Every rotten thing that had happened
flashed before his eyes.

Suddenly, Hopper threw down the books.
THUMP!
Everyone in the library stared at Hopper.
Mrs. Pumpkin frowned.
"Hopper O'Hare, you need a time out,"
she said. "Please go to Sir Byron's office."

Chapter 3
The Rain Storm

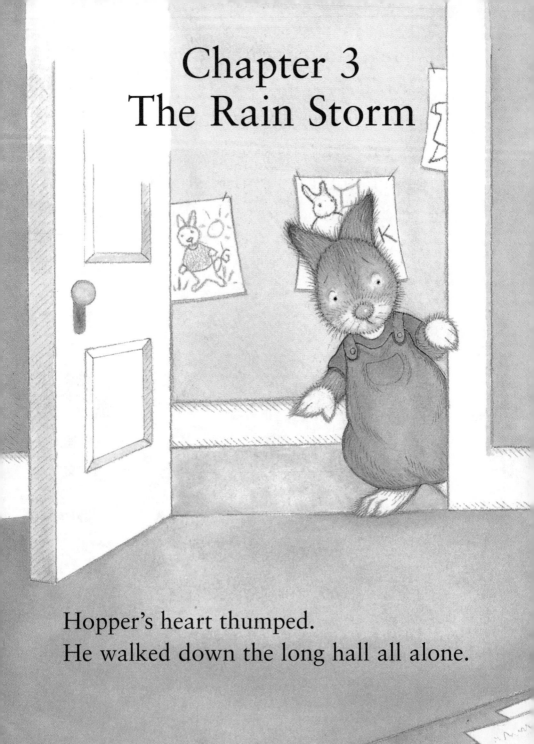

Hopper's heart thumped.
He walked down the long hall all alone.

Hopper had never been
to the principal's office!
Would Sir Byron yell at him?
Would he call his mother?
Would Hopper have to stay after school?

Hopper sat down in Sir Byron's office.
"Everyone gets angry sometimes,"
Sir Byron said. "When we get angry,
it feels like a storm inside us.
The sky gets dark.
Thunder BOOMS and lightning CRASHES.
And the rain pours down."
"I felt like that in the library!"
Hopper said.
Sir Byron smiled.

"But when the storm ends,
there is a rainbow," Sir Byron said.
Hopper looked out the window.
The clouds were gone.
The storm was over.
"Look!" Hopper said.
"There's a rainbow!"

Chapter 4
A Happy Bunny

"Are you ready to go back to class?"
Sir Byron asked.
Hopper nodded.
He felt as calm as the sky.

He felt a lot better.
He knew other storms would come.
But he also knew they would pass.

The next day, Hopper brought
his library books to school.
"I'm sorry I lost my temper yesterday,"
he told Mrs. Pumpkin.
The librarian smiled.
"Everyone gets angry sometimes,"
she said.

Then she took out a stack of books.
"I saved these for you," she said.
His books!
Hopper smiled.

Hopper thanked Mrs. Pumpkin.
Then he hopped down the hall
back to class.